HIS Other JOB

his other job

MILA HART

EDITED BY
WALLFLOWER EDITS

COVER BY
VANILLA LILY DESIGNS

SALVATORE

"LISTEN TO ME, SALVATORE." My father started speaking, and, by the tone of his voice, I could tell it was a serious topic. Lines of worry were etched into his expression, making him appear older than his actual age, and his eyes held something I'd never seen before— doubt, hesitation maybe. He ran a hand through his thinning hair and let out a slow sigh. "You're next in line to be the head of the family."

I didn't know where this was going, but the amount of time it was taking him to spit out whatever he had to say let me know it couldn't be good.

"But how am I supposed to entrust you

with such a huge responsibility when you've yet to take a wife of your own?"

I wanted to roll my eyes, punch the wall, scream about the injustice of this archaic mentality, but instead, I held my tongue. This wasn't the first time he'd brought this up, but the hardness in his stare that I'd mistaken for doubt or hesitation was, in fact, neither. He was tired of having this discussion—there was no mistaking this would be the last time this came up.

"I don't seem to be able to impress upon you the importance of our family lineage, our heritage. But it's not just about history, Salvatore. It's about the family's future. We would be the laughingstock of the community if it turned out you couldn't carry on our family name. And not with just *any* girl, but a good girl, one who would make me proud and, in turn, be a good, strong partner for you to have at your side."

"Yes, sir." The words came out in obedience and respect, but that didn't mean I was happy about uttering them.

In total transparency, I didn't believe in romance or any of the bullshit that came with it. It was nothing but a fairy tale mothers told their daughters when they didn't want them to think they would end up alone, a lie propagated by Disney and Hallmark to sell movies and cards. It was all a fabrication of fiction, plain and simple. And the rare ones who did find something akin to it ended up with a liability, not just a wife. In our line of work—my line of work—having people the enemy knew you loved, innocents, was nothing more than a hazard.

But I also knew that not finding someone to fill a role my father believed was vital to the family would be essentially forfeiting what I had worked so hard for my entire life. I was the best person to be in charge when he stepped down, but I wouldn't be able to show that if I didn't follow my father's advice, even as foolhardy as I believed it was.

Finding a woman wouldn't be difficult. That much was a given. I wasn't cocky, but I was certainly confident. And I knew I was quite the catch. Even if I weren't good-looking, the wealth attached to my last name would be more than enticing. Fortunately for me, I had both. Any woman would be lucky to have me.

The perks that came with being part of my family seemed to be enticing for any female I came in contact with. But at this point, I was beyond thinking I'd find "the one"—since I didn't believe in that shit anyhow. I was now in a position to find "the one I can tolerate." And once I found her, I planned on that being the end of it.

If my father had taught me one thing, it was that love didn't have to play a role in every marriage. Some of the best relationships did not involve such a useless emotion, especially in a family like ours. The best thing I could do was find a woman who knew her place, played her part, and left me alone to do my job. It would be a marriage of convenience—nothing more, nothing less. Besides, it wasn't like I would be using them in the slightest. They'd have plenty of advantages being with me, having my last name. She would reap the benefits of being a Romano, and I would get my title and my father off my back. It would be a win for us both.

My father opened his mouth, likely to say something else before our car was jostled and the sound of crumbling metal rattled my ears.

My eyes widened as the old man was thrown against the door, pressed up against it. My immediate thought was one of the many enemies we'd made over the years had made an attempt on our lives.

"Stay here." I quickly exited the vehicle without waiting for my father's reply, crouching behind the door, and scanned the perimeter of the car for threats.

He was the best leader our family had ever seen, but age had made him slow, and attacks called for quick thinking and even faster moving. If this were an enemy, I needed to be the one to deal with it. My dad didn't look pleased with the command, but he didn't argue, either.

With a gun pressed against my hip, I crept around the hood of the sedan, ready to use it. My heart thudded in my chest as my adrenaline kicked in. But as I looked around, I couldn't locate a threat or even any angry bystander. It wasn't an enemy from a rival family at all. When I realized it was merely a fender bender, I stood up straight and eased my hand off my 9mm, allowing my jacket to fall over it, covering the firearm.

It was a girl.

Beautiful, sweet, somewhat broken, and a tad bit disheveled.

I couldn't pinpoint what it was about the girl, but in that moment, I forgot everything I'd ever believed about the opposite sex. Maybe it was her eyes, or possibly her gorgeous hair, or it could have even been the distressed look on her face—whatever it was, all I could think about was her.

Every warning bell and flag my nervous system could send off was sounding and waving in an attempt to get me to retreat, but the connection was instant, the pull irresistible —magnetic. She was like the latest, greatest toy at Christmas that I hoped Santa would bring or my parents had sprung for. The only difference now was that I didn't have to depend on someone else to bring me the finer things in life. When I wanted something, I took it. I wanted her—in what capacity I couldn't be certain—and I wouldn't stop until I had her.

one

ABBY

FUCK! My life couldn't get any worse right now. Every time things started to look up, something happened to mess that all up. Life, Karma, Mother Nature—whoever—just wouldn't cut me a break. Every damn time I took one step forward, life pushed me two steps back. I was sick of constantly being the one who ended up with the absolute worst luck.

I glanced down at the clock when I finally walked into the building where I worked—fifty-two minutes late. All I could do was hope the boss wasn't there today, or maybe he'd be in a meeting. That was the only way my tardiness would be overlooked. And what were the chances of that happening? *Slim*. Why? *Because the ruler of the universe hated me.*

I forced myself not to think about the people staring at me as I walked through the reception area, trying to get to my office on the nineteenth floor. Like high school students, they were snickering at my misfortune. In the midst of the accident this morning, I'd managed to dump an entire cup of coffee down my shirt which had stained it and made my white blouse nearly transparent. And with the cooler temperature of the morning and wet clothing, everyone could see my bra and the peaks beneath it. *It was going to be a fabulous day at work.*

I forged ahead, ignoring their whispers, and once I got to my office, I closed the door with a heavy sigh. I wished I were one of those women who prepared for everything. The type who kept a change of clothes in her bottom desk drawer for just such an occasion, but no such luck. I was lucky to make it through each day by the skin of my teeth. I certainly didn't have anything to change into, and as late as I already was, there wasn't much I could do about it. I definitely didn't have time to run home to change, which meant I'd have to suck it up and deal with it...for the rest of the day.

The coffee and the clothes were just the icing on the cake. I had no clue how I'd managed the travesty that was my morning. I had no idea how I'd managed to ram right into that car—that expensive-ass luxury sedan. It was so rare that I didn't even know what type of car it was, and I didn't recognize the logo. It never failed. I owned a hunk of junk made when steel was still the primary choice for automobile manufacturers, leaving it with nothing more than a few scratches. It was so ancient that nothing could break that old girl. His car, however, did not fare so well in the collision. It had crumpled like a tin can under a hammer and probably cost more than I'd make in a lifetime. Go figure. With my luck, the next thing on my agenda would be a lawsuit. *Kill me now.* I groaned at the mere thought.

And then I remembered just how stupid I'd come across when the man had gotten out of his car. I'd been struck dumb by his beauty—yes, *beauty*. A man shouldn't be that gorgeous, but that one was. Thick, dark hair, stunning green eyes, and the perfect blend of muscle and height—if Adonis had been Italian, this man could have been his twin. I'd been so in awe of the magnificence before me that I hadn't spoken a word. Nothing. Zilch. Zip. Nada. Like I was mute, I had just stared at him, memorizing every detail because I knew I'd never see anything—or rather anyone—so gorgeous again in my lifetime. I'd heard of deer in the headlights but never pertaining to attraction...and my God, was it obvious I was attracted...or stupid. It could go either way. When I realized how long he'd been talking to me before I had responded, I wanted to slap myself upside the head but figured that would just make it worse.

Without a doubt, he was the most stunning man I'd ever seen—hands down. Italian, masculine, a sharp jawline with a dusting of scruff, and a dimple in his left cheek. But it was those eyes—they were intense and the greenest green I'd ever seen.

I looked down at the business card he had handed me. *Salvatore Rossi*. His name was as intriguing as his appearance. And damn, I wanted to call the guy, but not for the reasons I was supposed to. I needed to contact him about fixing his car, not his fixing my libido.

After what I had been through, the last thing I needed to be thinking about was a man. The last relationship I'd been in had left me relentlessly abused, scarred, and bruised. Justin had taught me an important lesson— not everything is always what it seems. I'd learned that and wasn't the slightest bit interested in rushing into another situation where I'd learn another equally painful life lesson. It had taken me years, two lawyers, and untold time in court to get out of that. No, thank you.

Justin had ruined me for other men. There wasn't much I could do to change that, but I could learn from it. Those scars ran deep, a hell of a lot deeper than surface level, and they hid in places where other people couldn't see them. And thinking about it would only resurrect memories I was desperate to evade. I'd escaped with my life, but he'd left behind a hell of a lot of damage I couldn't get rid of.

But time had allowed my mind to enjoy some of the little pleasures a day threw at me. Despite the car accident, the coffee, and the blouse, I could still appreciate a fine man. That, however, was where it would stop. I would look. I might even smile. And in this case, I'd probably think about him from time to time. But it had to end there. My thoughts would go nowhere. I wouldn't act on an impulse to accept a dinner invitation or even flirt with someone of the opposite sex—I couldn't. The only thing I would do was wish things were different—that my past wasn't quite as tainted.

Despite what the American public believes with their cancel culture, history can't be changed. It was what it was—good, bad, or indifferent. I chose to learn from my mistakes instead of pretending like they hadn't happened.

Everything about that man—Salvatore—screamed danger. And it wasn't just a little warning. It was a big, red flag waving right in my face. We were not the same, clearly. We didn't come from the same walks of life. It was evident he came from money, privilege. And me...I was a hot mess on a good day, and we didn't need to mention which side of the tracks I'd stumbled across.

I needed to stay far, far away from a man

who exuded any kind of danger, much less one who radiated it in waves. I didn't want to end up getting myself hurt and be the next big headline on the news. But, then again, the last man I'd dated had been the safe choice—or so I'd thought. He had been my best bet, and even he'd had some skeletons in his closet that nobody had expected, like using women for punching bags. "Safe" clearly hadn't landed me in a great position in that case.

The more I thought about the Italian god, the more I fantasized about what it would be like to know him, be involved with him. Maybe, I needed a bit of danger in my life—a risk, something to make my heart race. Salvatore could be just that. Or, he would be if that were what I was looking for. No. No. No. I couldn't even entertain that idea. For the foreseeable future, I didn't need a man in my life in any capacity—safe or dangerous. I was sure about that. Or I thought I was. Hell, the truth was I wasn't sure about anything in my life other than whatever could go wrong would.

SOMEONE KNOCKED ON MY DOOR, interrupting my thoughts about Salvatore, and I nearly groaned at the loss.

I cleared my throat and sat up straighter in my chair. "Come in," I said, keeping my voice clear and loud.

The doorknob jiggled before it opened, and my boss, Bradley, walked inside. He dwarfed my tiny office. "Abby," he began, and I mentally prepared myself for the tongue lashing I was about to receive. His eyebrows knitted, and his lips turned down as he took in my tousled appearance. "What is that all over your shirt?"

I peeked down at my blouse, praying it had

dried enough that my boss couldn't still see my lingerie or my nipples. "Coffee." I hoped he wouldn't ask for any more information.

No such luck.

"And why are you wearing your coffee?" His eyes darted to my chest before they met mine again. "You understand you're out of dress code, don't you?"

"Yes, sir," I answered. "But I don't have anything to change into—"

"I'll have Avery pick up something for you."

"That's not necessary but thank you. I'll just stay in my office with my head down, working until the end of the day."

Bradley seemed distracted before he remembered why he'd come in here. "Oh, Abby…You were almost an hour late this morning?"

I took a deep breath and admitted my morning had been worse than just the spill on my outfit. "Yes. I was in a car accident."

Bradley glanced out the window. "Your car looks fine."

I wasn't sure how he could make that determination since my car wasn't visible out the window from the nineteenth story of the high-rise we worked in, but instead of mentioning that, I decided to go with something a bit more lighthearted instead. "You should see the other guy's." I snickered nervously.

He didn't seem to get that it was a bit of a joke. "Are you okay?"

I probably wasn't in the best mental state, but I knew that wasn't what my boss wanted to hear. It also wasn't a direct result of the accident so much as who I'd hit. So, I nodded instead. "For the most part, I think I'm fine."

I'd never believed employers really cared about the truth or my personal life. They really only wanted to hear that nothing would ever affect your job performance and that you'd make up missed time. It was all about the bottom line—profit. My words were a lie far from the truth. I wasn't fine, but that didn't have anything to do with the car accident or my employment, so I kept it to myself.

"That's good to hear." Bradley leaned against my desk. "Your performance these last few days has been nothing short of phenomenal. The company wants to thank you for all the hard work you've done. I'm certainly grateful for all you do."

My cheeks heated, and in turn, I knew they had started to pinken as well. I wasn't an attention-seeking person, and compliments always flattered me *and* embarrassed me, especially when I wasn't prepared for them. Today, I not only wasn't prepared, but I'd also been expecting an ass-chewing for being late.

I smiled and shifted in my chair. "I'm happy to hear that, and it only makes sense to do my best for a company as exceptional as this one." That even sounded like canned bull-shit to me, so I couldn't imagine how it had come across to Bradley. I wanted to roll my eyes but managed to keep them trained on his face.

I needed him to get to the point of his pres-ence or make a swift exit. In addition to the car accident, my daydreaming had put me even further behind. Bradley was not helping the situation. When I glanced at the clock, I almost cried, knowing how much I had left to accom-plish and how little time I had to do it in. Mindlessly thinking about a stranger I'd likely never see again was hardly a reason to get stuck at the office late. I brought my thoughts back to the man in front of me and wondered why he was still lingering. I assumed the only reason for his appearance was to get an excuse for my being late. But he was still looming in my doorway.

My eyes met his, and I looked him over—really *looked* him over. He was cute, that was for sure. With blond hair and blue eyes, he had that boy-next-door appeal, and to most women, I would imagine he was considered an attractive guy. But after seeing Salvatore, I couldn't imagine ever thinking anyone else was attractive again. I shook my head just a bit, trying to rid myself of all things Salvatore. I kept reminding myself that I didn't want anything to do with men, especially not a nice one who reminded me of my ex-husband, which Bradley certainly did.

He cocked his head to the side just slightly, almost imperceptibly. "You do remember there's a company picnic after work today, right?"

I'd completely forgotten about that. Had I remembered, I would have had a change of clothes to attend. As it was, I would have to figure out a way to leave early—hard to do since I was late and currently behind—so I could change and not make the owner think I was an absolute slob when I met him for the first time.

I nodded as if I'd known all along. "Thank you for reminding me."

"Of course." He smiled, leaving me with a feeling that there was more he wanted to say that he just kept to himself.

I wasn't surprised, but I also didn't question it. For the last couple of months, I'd gotten the impression Bradley had a crush on me. He did everything he could to make my life easier, things he didn't do for his other employees. Bradley took special care to remind me of events and ask how I was doing in the morning. But it was something more. I couldn't quite pinpoint it, but there was more there...on his part.

He was a great guy, just not the guy for me.

"I'll leave you to work then, and if you need anything, just let me know."

"I will. Thank you."

He tapped his hand on the doorjamb, hesitating before he exited. "I'll send you the details for the picnic."

I already had them, but I nodded to appease him anyway. "Sounds great." "I'll see you there."

"Yep."

Bradley left my office with something on his mind—or maybe his agenda—but I ignored the obvious and got back to work, fully immersing myself. By diving in and skipping lunch, I managed to catch up an hour before quitting time. I doubled checked my to-do list and quickly scanned my email.

Just like he'd said he would, Bradley had sent me the email about the company picnic. A company-wide email had gone out a week or so ago if I wasn't mistaken, so I wasn't sure why he would have thought I hadn't gotten it, regardless of the fact that I had forgotten about it.

I quickly scanned the email. I was a bit hesitant before I gathered the courage to respond.

Good afternoon, Bradley,

I know it's not customary, but I would like to see if you have any objections to my leaving early? I have completed everything I had to do today and need to run home to change clothes. I don't want to meet the owner of the company and appear unprofessional in my current state of undress. Please let me know if that would be all right.

The response came within minutes, much quicker than I had anticipated.

That will be fine, Abby. We will see you at the picnic.

I took that as my cue to leave and raced home. I slipped out of the stained clothes and ran myself a hot shower. I wouldn't be able to relax in it like I wanted to, but at least I would be able to get myself cleaned up and presentable.

After I was out of the shower, I changed into an appropriate but cute red summer dress, which seemed acceptable because of how hot it would be outside, despite the sun beginning to set. I debated whether I should add makeup or not before figuring a little bit never hurt. I always aired on the side of natural anyhow.

I pulled my hair into a ponytail and then rushed out of the house to get to the picnic. I looked much more presentable, and I felt even better now that I didn't have a huge coffee stain highlighting my breasts and showcasing my bra.

The picnic was in full swing by the time I arrived. Several of my coworkers were conversing with one another when I stepped out of my car. I wasn't really very close to anyone I worked with. Actually, I didn't talk to any of them at all. I kept to myself for the most part. My life was typically bland but not in a bad way. It was a choice I'd made after all I'd been through with Justin. Simple tended to mean less drama which equated to fewer headaches and heartaches. It also led to a tinge of loneliness and isolation, but that was the price I was willing to pay not to endure any repeats of past mistakes.

I'd planned to make polite conversation, but no sooner had I gotten near the party than my stomach rumbled—loudly. I found myself bypassing my coworkers and heading straight to the food. I hadn't eaten all day, and I needed something to snack on. I tried not to make it obvious that I was on a direct path to nourishment as I nodded and greeted some of my coworkers before reaching the table.

In my haste to stop my growling hunger, I

hadn't paid much attention to anyone once I'd passed the group of people who worked on my floor. I beelined straight for the bags of chips, grabbing a bag at the same time someone else did.

I snatched my hand away as I looked up with a casual smile. "Oops." My eyes widened, and my heart stopped.

There, before me, was the Italian god from this morning. Dark. Handsome. Dangerous.

Salvatore.

Could my luck get any worse?

three

NOTHING I DID WAS EVER by coincidence. Nothing that ever happened to me was by coincidence. I hadn't let chance dictate when I would see her again. I had taken matters into my own hands because when you left things to fate, it had a funny way of screwing things up.

I knew exactly where she was going to be and when—thank you, Bradley—and I had arranged for an opportunity to "bump" into her. As creepy as it sounded, it wasn't because I wanted to steal her away or lock her in some basement. On the contrary, I wanted to cherish this woman like she was the only one in the world. I had no idea why and wondered if maybe I had hit my head when she'd rammed into us.

As cliché as it sounded, the second I laid eyes on her, I knew I was screwed. I didn't believe in love, much less love at first sight. Yet, here I was, at a company picnic, forcing an encounter with a woman who'd completely consumed my thoughts since I'd laid eyes on her roughly nine hours earlier. It wasn't rational. It wasn't sane. But I saw something I wanted and I'd moved heaven and earth in a short amount of time to make it happen.

I was a man with principles, and I was stubborn. When I made up my mind about something, it was rare that I changed it for any reason. Love was one of those things. But life had thrown me a curveball to make me rethink everything I thought I believed in. It helped that I had an army of men at my disposal to orchestrate all that had taken place today for me to proceed. Thankfully, there was nothing any of them had dug up that prevented me from searching out my little flower, not that they could have come up with much that would have changed my mind or dissuaded me.

Love at first sight was real—I was a believer now—and it was exactly how I felt about this girl. I didn't care if someone thought it was a chemical imbalance or wanted to have me committed. My mind was made up. I would marry this woman and make her mine if it was the last thing I did. I hoped, for both of us, that it didn't come down to that. I wanted her to come willingly. It wouldn't have the same appeal if I had to force her hand...but I wasn't above it.

All I could think about was how gorgeous she'd looked. Yes, she was an absolute mess but a beautiful mess. *My* beautiful mess—whether she knew it or not. At the time, she'd had coffee dripping down her chest, soaked through the pale-white blouse she had been wearing. Her pencil skirt had been a bit torn, and the poor thing looked like she couldn't have been having a worse day.

But that was what had made her so perfect. Everything about her was so genuine, a trait not often found in the women in my circle. I couldn't help but want this woman. It didn't matter what detail I looked at; I was inspired, driven, desperate to have her. Her wavy, dirty-blond hair rolled down her shoulders like a waterfall, and her eyes were this rich brown that would catch the attention of everyone in the room—they were so bold and big, filled with expression, emotion. And her olive skin was total perfection—the stuff makeup commercials were made of. But every time I thought about her, which I did a lot since her running into us, I dreamed about how perfectly she'd fit in the crevice of my arm. She was tiny, delicate like a flower.

She was perfect, and she was mine.

After meeting her, no matter how unconventional it might have been, I had one of the only men I trusted with my life, Lukas, do a background search on her, and then his team did their thing without knowing who or what it was for. Together, they drew up a detailed file the FBI would drool over. I wanted to know everything there was to know about this woman before I dived in and tried to claim her. I needed to know how she'd grown up, her fears, what she enjoyed doing. Hell, I wanted to know where she bought her socks and who did her hair. Every single detail mattered.

I only got one chance to make a second impression, after all, and it had to be perfect.

By the time Lukas and his team were finished, I was greedy, ready to look into the inner workings of her life and see everything she had going on. I hoped she wasn't married, but even if she were, that wouldn't stop me from being with her. We'd just have to get rid of her husband. It wasn't a pretty part of the lifestyle I led, but it happened, and I wouldn't have been the one who got my hands dirty anyway.

Thankfully, she wasn't married so that possible was mess was avoided. Divorced. I hadn't expected that from someone so young. Abby Forbes was only twenty-four. What had made her think that she was ready to get married? Hopefully, she wasn't a compulsive person; otherwise, our relationship would be a rocky one.

I had to make sure the ex was no longer in the picture, either of his own accord or that of my men. I wasn't picky; he just had to be gone.

As I read further in the file, that question was answered for me.

Her ex-husband, Justin Forbes, was currently serving time in prison for abusing his wife—my flower. I bristled with the fury that he had dared to lay a hand on my precious woman. Prison was too good for him, compared to what I would do.

I WASN'T A GOOD MAN, far from it. And while I kept that part of my life on the down-low, I didn't mind who I was. I did what had to be done, which was important, especially in my line of work. It was what had primed me for being at the head of the family next. Being nice or good would get me thrown into a ditch on the side of the road or an ocean with cement shoes. But despite what I did for a living, I would never let out my frustrations or anger on a child or woman. Innocents went untouched—that was a hard line I didn't cross and neither did my men. And if a woman *had* to be dealt with, which happened from time to time, we had other women who handled that piece of the family business. Men did not lay a finger on a woman out of aggression—not in my family or my employ.

Men like that were beneath dirt, lower than pond scum, and I hated them, detested them with every fiber of my being. This Justin guy was a disgrace to all males, and someone like him didn't deserve the chance to be with a woman like Abby, anyway. I could only imagine how she felt about it all and the memories that haunted her. A woman who had played the hand life had dealt her had to be guarded, paranoid. There was no way she didn't live every day in some form of agony. It wasn't possible for her to just shake off the things her husband had done—I'd read the court reports in horrific detail—but I would do my best to help her figure out a way.

I was going to make it all the better for her.

There wasn't a single ounce of me that felt bad about ordering the hit on Justin. I didn't hesitate or even think twice about it. For what he'd done, he was lucky it would be a quick and easy death rather than having it long and drawn out. If he weren't in prison, I'd delight in being the one to deliver justice to the bastard by my very own hand. And I would make his suffering endure for longer than he believed he could handle, then I'd bring him back only to dole out more. Fucker.

But I had other things to focus on. Justin would be dealt with in prison, and Abby would never have to worry about his release. The only ground he'd see again would be the soil he was buried six feet under. Her freedom from her past would come in less than twenty-four hours' time, whether she knew it or not.

My only goal today was to *talk* to Abby. Now that I knew her past, I had to tread lightly. A woman like her, who had endured the abuse she had at the hands of someone who "loved" her, would no doubt be leery of relationships and men in general. In fact, she probably wasn't at all interested in any type of relation-ship with someone of the opposite sex. I'd have to take my time, win her over, get her to trust me. She'd have to see what I'd felt the moment I laid eyes on her and trust it was real, that she was safe, that I'd protect her at all costs.

I needed her to see that she wanted me as much as I wanted her... without sending up warning signals that would have her running in the opposite direction. The last thing I needed was for her to think I wasn't safe or trustworthy.

It was a delicate situation.

If any of this seemed planned, she would run like a mouse being chased by a cat without giving me a chance. Besides, what would I possibly say?

"Hey, I know this is weird, but the moment you crashed into my car, I fell in love with you. Oh, and I started stalking you because I knew we were meant to be together. Wanna get hitched?" Yeah. No. None of that was going to happen.

This wasn't some damn chick flick or a silly romantic comedy. I wasn't about to change everything about myself to impress a woman. I was who I was. Like me or not. But I would change my approach if it meant I got to be with her for the rest of my life.

As fate would have it, luck was on my side. What better way to organize a run-in than to own the company she worked for? Happenstance. Serendipity. Forced encounter. Control. Whatever you wanted to call it—the stars had aligned for a reason, and I planned to capitalize on the opportunity. But I had to do so casually. I couldn't talk to my dad about it because I had a feeling he would reject the idea. She wasn't from the mafia and, in his eyes, wouldn't be considered a good fit. Abby wouldn't have any idea what our life was like, much less what her role would be in our family. But maybe that was a good thing.

Seven or eight hours ago, I would have thought purchasing the company she worked for would have been an in-depth endeavor within itself. I had no idea the continued good fortune I'd have surrounding Abby, but while I was having it, I kept rolling with it—even if it cost me a small fortune. She worked for a mid-sized publishing company, nothing too big or serious, but they managed to turn a pretty decent profit, especially for their size.

In less than six hours, Lukas had put together a file on the company, gotten their financials, and I was able to have one of our lawyers draft an offer for the business. I had assumed the initial offer would be rejected, and I would find a price that the owner, Jeffrey Michaelson, liked. The business wasn't even on the market when my lawyer had approached the guy. Most entrepreneurs would have seen that as an opportunity to raise the selling price exponentially. I wanted it. He had it. And I was willing to pay cash—today. But, to my surprise, he accepted the offer and signed on the dotted line this afternoon without any further negotiation.

After the deal had been completed, I found out that his wife had been diagnosed with cancer, and he needed the money to get her the necessary treatment. Sad story but not my problem.

The second the money hit Jeffrey's account, he wished me luck and then left, trusting the company to my capable hands without so much as glancing back or an offer to train me or help me get my feet wet. It was amazing how fast cash could make things happen, but this was fast even with the kind of money I was used to.

SALVATORE

I DIDN'T KNOW MUCH about running a company, but I knew what it meant to be a leader. I was about to run the most powerful family in the Northeast. I hardly needed the money this company would put into my pocket. But I would do anything for Abby—I was borderline obsessed—and when our relationship blossomed, she'd feel much better knowing her significant other owned the company.

It was pure luck—something I didn't usually believe in—that they were having a company picnic the day I took over. All day, I'd been thinking of ways to see her, then we were able to make the sale happen like it was a divine plan, heaven directed. And as the new owner, this made everything so much easier. I didn't have to have an elaborate plan. All I had to do was attend the picnic, introduce myself to all of my new employees, and everything would fall into place from there.

It would all come together because I wouldn't let it end any other way.

I made sure to dress well. It was obvious to anyone who looked at my clothing that I had money, and I knew Abby found me attractive. It was obvious by the way she had stared at me when I'd gotten out of the car after the wreck. At first, I'd thought she might have had a concussion because nothing seemed to register when I talked to her, but then, I realized she was awestruck. If I weren't mistaken, I'd even seen a little bit of drool coming from the corner of her mouth. But the feeling had been mutual; she just hadn't known it.

I wasn't left waiting at the picnic for long when I finally saw the raggedy car Abby drove pull into the parking lot. Once we were together, the first thing I would do was get her a car that would keep her safe, rather than that hunk of junk that was who knows how old.

When she stepped out of the vehicle, heads turned toward her. Every man here ogled Abby, but it was obvious she either didn't see it or didn't reciprocate the attention. Her red dress swayed as she moved, and God, if she wasn't the most beautiful thing I'd ever seen. My dick twitched in my pants, and I had to let out deep breaths to keep it from being a full-blown erection. I hardly cared about what other people would think, but I didn't want Abby to believe I merely wanted her for her body. That was certainly enticing, but I wanted it all.

To say that I didn't want her was a blatant lie. I couldn't look at her and not want her, quite frankly. There was nothing I'd rather do than to pin her against the bed and thrust myself so deep into tight pussy that she could feel me in her stomach. But we could ease into that part—it would come sooner than she expected; that I could promise. For now, I just wanted to be close to her, smell her, get to know her. Anything she'd give me.

I excused myself from the mundane conversation around me that I hadn't been participating in anyhow and moved as she did. Her trajectory seemed to shift, and her hand went to her stomach. As she went for the food, so did I.

I made my way over to the table and intentionally reached for the same bag of chips she had her hand on. The apparent shock when she recognized me was priceless. I wish I would have been able to take a picture. Immediately, an apologetic expression came over her face.

"Salvatore," she started. She ripped her hand away from the bag. "What are you doing here?" Abby looked around like she was the butt of a joke or was somehow being punked. "You don't work here, do you?"

"Not until this morning. I just bought the company." I hadn't meant to say it with the arrogance it came off with, but she seemed to miss the part about my just having purchased the business.

Her eyes widened. "You're the owner?"

A smirk danced at the corner of my lips. "I am."

"And I hit you with my car." She looked distraught. "I'm such an idiot."

It took everything I had not to scold her for talking about herself that way. I wanted to say something, but I wouldn't, not now, anyway. "You're not an idiot. It was an accident."

"I still have your card." She pulled it out of her purse and showed it to me. "I was going to call you, I swear. I was late to work, then we had this picnic tonight, and I had to go home and change before coming here. But I'm not a hit and run type of person." Panic was written all over her face.

I never thought she was. She was far too angelic to ever be that kind of person.

"I believe you." I kept my voice calm and cool, like I didn't have a care in the world other than talking to this sweet angel in front of me.

Her chest heaved with anxiety and likely panic. "I can pay for all of the damages."

On what salary? "Don't worry about it."

"Was there anyone else in the car with you?"

I shrugged, trying not to make this a big deal. I didn't want her to feel guilty. "Just my dad."

She gasped. "Is he okay?" She tightened her ponytail, and when she did, her dress gaped at her cleavage, giving me a hint of what I'd find underneath that fabric.

My cock stirred again, but I was able to adjust my pants without notice.

"He's not...dead, is he?"

It seemed a bit extreme that she thought we would have exchanged numbers, not called the police or an ambulance, and her think he was anything other than fine. I laughed. "He's alive and well. Stop panicking, okay? If something were wrong, you would know."

Abby nodded. "At least let me take care of the damages, okay?"

"How about this?" Here was my opportunity. "Instead of worrying about the car or the damages, how about giving me the honor of having dinner with me?"

It wasn't as blunt as I'd normally be, but I needed to give her time to get used to that side of me. When we were together, she wasn't going to have a choice but to accept that. Abby appeared shocked at my request and fiercely bit into her bottom lip. It was a turn-on for me, and I had to look away from her for a second so I didn't give in to my urges and take her in front of all of my employees and her coworkers.

"I don't know..." The sheepish look on her

face again made me want to beat the hell out of her ex. "I'm just getting out of a really bad relationship." Her gaze fell to her feet at her half-truth. She had been divorced for over a year, but the court case had recently ended, landing her ex in prison.

I gently reached out to tip her chin up with my fingers. "I'm not asking you to jump into another one." I paused, giving her the chance to see the truth in my eyes and hopefully gain a little trust. "I just want to spend time with you, get to know you."

Abby was silent for a moment, thinking about it before she nodded. I could only assume that my position in the company had afforded me a level of trust I hadn't earned.

"Okay."

WHEN WAS the last time I went on a first date? When was the last time I'd gone on a date at all? Justin and I had met in middle school, been in a relationship for almost eight years, married for two of those. In the beginning, he used to take me out all the time, but that had changed as soon as there was a ring on my finger.

We had been high school sweethearts, and he was the only man I'd ever been with in any capacity. I hadn't seen the signs, and, in the end, that was what had gotten me in trouble. But how would I have known as someone who'd only ever been with one man? No one else in my life saw anything wrong, either, at least not before it was too late.

It was in the past now, and I liked the past to stay firmly rooted there. I had no plans to repeat the same mistakes, and I was determined to be strong and not to let my history affect my future. I would be able to live a normal life where I wasn't known as the wife whose husband had abused her. I was Abby Forbes, and I was okay.

Considering I hadn't been on a date in eight years, I was going to be rusty. I tried to think about what I'd done back then, but it was much harder said than done. Nothing came to mind, and it was far too late to attempt to call one of my friends to see what they said. I was going to have to wing it and do the best I could.

I would be rusty, but I was going to do it. I hadn't really wanted to go out with anyone anyhow, so whatever happened happened. If I crashed and burned, who cared? And if it went great, then I was worried about nothing. *C'est la vie.*

I couldn't help but wonder why Salvatore wanted to go on a date with me anyway. We'd only met two times, and they hadn't exactly been great experiences. I wasn't going to complain, but I did have questions. He was incredibly attractive, but what in the world did a man like him see in a woman like me? It would be impossible for him not to have his fair share of admirers. How could he not when he looked the way he did? Add in his wealth and I was surprised he wasn't covered in women hanging off his arms and waiting for his next word. The man could have any girl he wanted from any walk of life.

So, why was he picking me?

Even though it was way too early for me to be getting involved with another man, I was going to do this anyway. In all fairness, Justin had been behind bars for a while now, and I was using that as an excuse to keep my distance. Salvatore was the first man who'd been able to even get me to consider dating again, and I was going to make sure I looked hot while I did it. If this was a one-time thing, I wanted Salvatore to remember it as something incredible. I had to put the past behind me and just be me. At least for tonight.

I just couldn't get past the "why me" until I

started thinking about the odds of how it had all come to fruition. The likelihood of my hitting the new boss of my company were lottery-winning chances. This guy was the new owner of the company where I worked. Or rather, he was my boss's boss's boss. I was an incredibly safe driver, and the one time that I had hit someone, it would be my employer. What were the odds?

As soon as I'd seen him at the picnic, I'd been so afraid I was about to be fired on the spot, but Salvatore didn't seem to mind in the slightest. He must have been loaded with money because I'd hit him pretty hard. The car was totaled, and I felt like any other person would have been furious. But why would he be when he could easily buy himself a new one? Or maybe that was the reason he should be; weren't rich people assholes who only cared about themselves and amassing more wealth?

I turned on some music to drown out all my questioning thoughts while I went through my clothes in an attempt to find something to wear. I wanted to look sexy but not like a slut, which happened to be a very fine line. I didn't have many outfits to explore.

I had lost a lot when I'd left Justin, and I hadn't made replacing any of it a priority. I had enough to go to work and lounge around, but I really needed to make time to go shopping.

Finally, I settled on a navy-blue romper that fit me nicely. It was solid and made my breasts look fantastic, but I wasn't throwing them out there for everyone to take a look. There was a small sash, which I tied to high-light my hourglass figure. It was sexy but not terribly revealing, classy in a downplayed sort of way.

As I studied myself in the mirror, I realized that Salvatore hadn't told me what we were doing on this date of ours. I didn't know if we would be inside or out. And in terms of hair, it was better to be safe than sorry. So, I tied my hair in two French braids that hung down my back.

Again, I kept the makeup simple. I always preferred a more natural look, especially because it made me different from who I used to be. Justin had always liked my face totally painted and my body in the most revealing clothes he could find. He kept the scars covered, and he never left bruises where they could be counted.

I thought he did it to show me off, to show everyone what he had that they didn't. I'd never realized how much of a bragger Justin was before we said, "I do." I wouldn't say I liked that side of my ex-husband but mentioning something to him about it was how I would end up using concealer the next day to cover my black eye.

Shaking off thoughts of Justin and my past life, I focused on the present. It was my time now. I used minimal foundation and concealer and then a bit of mascara to make my eyelashes as long as possible. With a small amount of blush added, I figured I looked good enough to say I'd made an effort without being so flashy that I'd draw attention.

And just in time to I hear a knock on my door.

I SLID on some sandals and walked over to the front door. When I opened it, Salvatore was standing there. He had on a dark suit with an even darker shirt. His hair was pushed back, and those dreamy eyes were staring at me like I was the only other person in the world. I bit into my bottom lip, unable to believe just how irresistible he was.

It should be illegal for any man to look that damn good. And then I caught a whiff of his cologne and about came undone.

I was, officially, going on a date with my boss, and it felt so right. Butterflies took flight in my stomach, and a funny sensation tingled between my legs that I hadn't felt in years.

"I trust your day has been good?" Salvatore raised an eyebrow as he stepped into the house.

He looked so big in such a small room. He had what appeared to be grocery bags in his hands, and my brows furrowed as I thought about what he was doing.

"It was. Thanks for asking." I closed the door after him. "What do you have?"

He held the bags up higher. "Our date."

I was totally lost. "What?"

Salvatore didn't answer. He merely smiled. "Where's your kitchen?"

I frowned before pointing in the direction he needed to go. He walked toward it with me following him like a curious kid, not that he seemed to mind. I was pretty sure I heard him chuckle.

He set the bags on the table before he started taking stuff out. Meat and other ingredients. What was he doing? Salvatore must have noticed how confused I was because he turned around to face me. "I'm going to cook dinner for you."

"You are?" I asked, my voice revealing how

shocked I was. I hadn't had anyone make me a meal in years.

Justin had always believed in the traditional gender roles and thought I should be the one in the kitchen. Thankfully, we never go to the barefoot and pregnant part. God knows how hard that would have made my life.

Salvatore was already proving that he was nothing like Justin. "Do you like lamb?"

I smiled, and my heart skipped a beat. "I love it."

It was very comfortable between Salvatore and me. Nothing was tense, and it felt like I had known him much longer than I had. Contrary to what I first had thought he would be like, he was very kind and funny. Easygoing. Spending time with him was far simpler than I had anticipated, and I found myself hoping this wouldn't be the last opportunity I was given to do so.

Once he'd plated the food and I'd set the table, we sat down together. It smelled fantastic, and the moment I took a bite, I couldn't keep my thoughts to myself. "The food is delicious," I wasn't lying; the man could cook. "I wasn't expecting this."

"What were you expecting?"

"I mean, you're rich." I shrugged and swallowed another bite of my dinner while he stared at me. "I didn't expect you to be able to cook. Don't you have people who do that for you?

Salvatore laughed as he sampled the lamb. "Well, I didn't expect this from you."

I cocked my head to the side, confused. "Expect what?"

"You to be so straightforward." He took a sip of wine and stared at me like he had more to say. "You seem so quiet."

"Looks can be deceiving." I smirked at him.

"I can tell." He sat back against his chair, wiped his mouth, and put his napkin back in his lap. "I have maids, yes, but my mother taught me how to cook before she passed. My food doesn't compare to hers in the slightest."

"I think she would be proud," I told him and reached my hand across the table to put it on top of his.

Salvatore stared at me for a long time with a blissful expression on his face. "I hope so." He smiled. "I should probably get going. As you can imagine, I have work in the morning, and I wouldn't want to impose on you."

"You're not imposing." It came out much quicker than it should have. My cheeks started to turn red, and I coughed. *Way to seem desperate, Abby.* "But, let me walk you out."

I stood up and was about to grab the plates before Salvatore beat me to it. He rolled up his sleeves and walked to the sink with the dirty dishes in his hands. He cleared the plates and rinsed them off before placing them into the dishwasher.

Could he be any more perfect? What man cooked and cleaned? Justin sure as hell hadn't.

When he was finished with the dishes, he put a hand on the small of my back, and we walked to the front door. He let me go and turned around so he could face me. "This is goodnight?"

I didn't want it to be. "Yes."

"Then, let's end this date the right way."

ABBY

MY BROWS RAISED IN CONFUSION, but Salvatore didn't leave me wondering what he meant for long. He put one hand delicately on my chin and leaned down to press his mouth to mine. It was gentle and easy, and I couldn't stop myself from kissing him back. His lips felt good on mine.

The kiss ended too quickly, and it left me wanting more. Salvatore pulled away slowly and looked into my eyes. There was something unspoken between the two of us, and while I didn't know what it was, I wasn't prepared to let him go.

I held onto his hand, not letting go of his fingers when he'd tried to separate. "Don't leave." My voice was soft and a bit breathy from the kiss, almost a plea instead of a request. "Stay with me." I had no idea where that had come from. *So much for not seeming desperate.*

Salvatore shook his head. "I like you too much, Abby. If I stay, I don't think I'll be able to keep my hands to myself."

"It's Abby," I corrected. I hadn't been called by my full name in a long time. I let my eyes drift down so I didn't have to see his face if he rejected me when I uttered the most forward words that had ever left my mouth. "And maybe I don't want you to keep your hands to yourself."

Salvatore clutched me against his body, pulling me tightly to his chest. He dipped his head next to my ear, and the warmth of his breath turned me on almost as much as his next words. "This is your last chance to say 'no.'"

"I don't need it."

Salvatore didn't say anything else. He didn't have to. His lips were back on mine, but this kiss was different. There was something behind it, and I had a feeling I knew exactly what it was. My mouth parted, welcoming his tongue and his affection. His hands roamed, as did mine, and nothing had ever felt more perfect, more sensual, more...right.

I shouldn't sleep with him, but the decision had already been made. I wanted him, and nothing was going to stop me.

Things escalated quickly between us. Salvatore pulled away from me, and his hands tugged at my romper before he turned me around, my chest against the wall so that he could unzip it and let it fall to the floor, pooling at my ankles.

Afterward, Salvatore picked me up, allowing me to wrap my legs around his waist. I left butterfly kisses all around his neck and didn't stop until he'd managed to find my room and threw me against the bed. I bounced on the mattress as he started to undress.

In the blink of an eye, his shirt slipped over the top of his head, and his pants found their way to the floor before he was back on top of me. Salvatore made quick work of my bra and threw it, uncaringly, into a corner in the room. He wrapped those magnificent lips around my breast and suckled, teasing my nipple with his tongue and teeth. My hands tangled in his hair, and I tugged on it relentlessly, pulling his lips back to mine. Salvatore felt better than good. It was electric, hedonistic—there was nothing I wouldn't do to bring this man pleasure.

He moved his lips to my neck and switched between sucking, kissing, and licking while his hips started to thrust against me. I didn't see him stopping any time soon, and God knew I didn't want him to. My hands clutched onto the sheets on my bed as he trailed his lips down until they reached my panties. They desperately needed to come off, sooner rather than later. I needed to feel him. Wanted to feel him. Craved having him inside me.

"There's no turning back from this?" He breathed against my hips.

I nodded in acceptance, unable to form words because of the pleasure he forced on me with every simple touch and every lingering kiss.

Salvatore didn't need verbal confirmation; he accepted my nod as all the consent he needed. He pulled my panties down my legs and began to feast between my thighs like it was the best thing he'd ever tasted. My eyes widened, and my lips separated. There was no stopping the moans and sighs from leaving my mouth. Every swirl, each lick, the non-stop warm breath against my delicate flesh...it was all too much.

I threw my head back and let out a deep groan. "Oh, Salvatore!"

"Yes, baby, I want to hear you. Scream for me!"

His tongue became more insistent. I tried to press my legs together, but Salvatore wasn't letting that happen. His hands pried my knees apart, spreading me open for him to continue to feast. My face contorted, and I almost felt like crying while I found a powerful climax I had been trying to stave off.

I struggled to catch my breath, but Salvatore didn't care. He ripped off his boxers and leaned over me before settling his hips between my thighs. I was wet from his indulgence, ready and waiting for him to slide in—deep. A gasp escaped my mouth as he growled from pure pleasure.

"I knew you would feel like this, baby girl,

and you're not disappointing me. You're the goddamn definition of perfection."

I didn't say anything. I couldn't. Salvatore started slowly enough, but he'd still stolen my ability to speak.

"I can't be gentle with you, Abby; I'm sorry." He kissed my neck.

That was the only warning I got before he was thrusting in and out of me in rapid succession. His hips moved against mine like he couldn't be sated until I felt another climax beginning to build inside of me.

Salvatore pulled out his long, thick cock and turned me around quicker than should have been possible. He held my hips, keeping me on my hands and knees, as he relentlessly fucked me from behind, harder than he'd done before with my moans egging him on.

"Oh God, Salvatore. I need to come!"

"Then, come."

A few more hard pumps and I couldn't contain myself or my voice that erupted as my muscles tensed and tightened in the most explosive orgasm I'd ever experienced, tumbling over the edge again, with Salvatore following after me.

nine

SALVATORE

WHEN I WOKE up the next morning, I was relaxed and calm, something I hadn't felt in a long time. When you were a part of a mafia, you didn't get to have a day off. But, with Abby, it felt like a day off in the best possible way. And I never wanted to let go of that feeling. It had happened so quickly—unnaturally so—but it had fully engulfed every part of me.

She was the best sex I'd ever had, and just one night with her was far from enough. As I looked at how beautiful she was while she slept, the only thing I could think about was how good she'd felt wrapped around me. It wasn't just being inside her; curled up with her was equally as addictive.

I wanted more—needed more.

With most women, one night was more than enough to get my fill. It was always just about sex. I didn't do relationships—ever. It led girls to think there was something more in store for them than there ever actually would be. But that wasn't the case with Abby. I'd always known she was special from the moment I'd locked eyes with her after she'd hit my car, but every minute I was in her presence, she proved it to me more and more.

Abby was much more than a one-night stand. She was the rest of my life which was what I'd known the second I'd shared space with her, standing in the middle of the road.

Little snores left her body, and I didn't want to disturb her. But I couldn't stop myself. She looked so heavenly, and every ounce of my being wanted to dirty her up. Besides, I had work that needed to be done, which couldn't be pushed back. That meant I didn't have much time to do what I wanted to do, and unfortunately, it wasn't on Abby's schedule.

I sat up and pushed down the covers,

pleased to see that she was still naked. Good. That was exactly how I wanted her. It made my job that much easier.

I found her pussy and slipped my tongue inside. She fidgeted but didn't wake up. My tongue lapped at her like she was my oasis in the middle of the desert, and it wasn't long before she started moaning, her eyes opening slowly to see what was going on.

She was confused, but she hardly had time to figure out what was happening before her hands were clutching the sheets fiercely. Her hips pushed upward, and she was trying to close her legs, attempting to nudge me away to manage her sensitivity. But I wasn't going to let her. I wanted her to take everything I was giving her and more.

And she did. "Salvatore," she moaned, and I spread her thighs apart to allow myself better and deeper access to her folds.

She tasted wonderful—sweet like candy— and I didn't ever want to stop tasting her. Shivers ran down her body, and goose bumps popped up all over her skin before she came, throwing her head back and moaning. It was a good thing she lived alone; otherwise, they would hear every single sound she was making and there was no disguising her pleasure. There was no keeping Abby quiet, and I didn't want to. I wanted to hear every peep she made.

Even after she'd come, I continued to lap at her clit and finger that pretty pink pussy of hers until Abby pushed away my face.

"I want you, Salvatore, please!" she begged, and when my baby girl wanted something, she was going to get it.

I would never withhold anything that was in my power to give her.

She squirmed in front of me, but I hadn't relented. My fingers still kept a steady rhythm to keep her engaged. "I need you."

"I know, baby." I withdrew my hand and licked my fingers before making eye contact with my lover. "I know."

I sat up, lifted her hips to meet mine, and thrust my dick deep inside of her. She gasped, but that didn't make me stop or even slow down. Once she had adjusted to my length, I forged ahead. Pillaging, plundering, searching for pleasure. Abby felt divine, wound so tight around me that I thought I was going to unravel. She was the only person who had ever been able to make me do that, to make me feel like this. It went beyond sex; it was euphoric.

The harder I pounded into her, the tighter she held onto me. Her nails dug into my skin, the most delicious bite I'd ever felt. I wanted to give her more to keep it coming.

"Salvatore, God!"

I pulled out and watched her face scrunch into a frown, disappointment obvious on her features. But I wasn't going to stop there. I was never going to stop. If she wanted me, then she was going to get me—all of me.

I turned Abby around on her hands and knees. It was a much deeper position, and when I pumped into her, I couldn't stop the groans leaving my mouth. She felt so much better this way, and I was going to get every bit of pleasure from this that I possibly could.

"Salvatore. Salvatore. Salvatore," she chanted as her orgasm overwhelmed her, leaving her breathless and unable to speak anything other than my name.

I'd never heard a better sound than my baby girl screaming out for me while she was fucked. She exploded around my cock, but that didn't stop me. No, she wasn't done until I had come inside that pretty pussy of hers.

My hips moved faster against her, slapping against her ass with every thrust. My fingers clawed into her hips, but she didn't seem to mind in the slightest. I was rough with her, but that seemed like it turned Abby on more than any gentleness I could have shown her.

With how tight she was, it was only a matter of time before reaching my climax. I continued, giving her everything I had and ensuring that she took in every last bit of my seed before I rested against her back, exhausted and panting.

ten

SALVATORE

ABBY WAS IT FOR ME. I never wanted anyone else—physically or emotionally. Our connection was something I couldn't identify. I couldn't define it. It just *was*. And it was never-ending.

I had to fuck her like there was no tomorrow—with me, there literally may not be. I had a dangerous occupation, and I lived in a world where every breath had a chance of being my last. With my job, my lifestyle, my family, I could be killed just as easily as I could kill. I'd always accepted that fact about being in the mafia, primarily because I didn't know anything different but especially since I was next in line to be the don. However, things were different now.

I had a reason to live and someone to return to. I was determined to come back to Abby, always. Which also made her a liability and me vulnerable. The moment word got out on the street that I had someone I cared about in my life, there would be a target on her back. A red dot that followed her everywhere she went, waiting for me to fuck up, for someone to take a shot to hurt me. But that was a reality I didn't want to face right now.

Once I had my breath back, I sat up and pulled out of her. Abby sighed and let her stomach hit the bed before turning over so she could face me. She was beautiful and flustered, and I wished I could look into those big, beautiful brown eyes for the rest of my life.

And I would.

"I have to go," I whispered to her, pushing a strand of hair out of her face.

Immediately, she started pouting, and my eyes went to those pouty, pink lips. She was so alluring, and I couldn't help but lean down and press my mouth against hers. Abby was eager to have me kiss her and wrapped her hands around my neck, pulling me closer to her although she wasn't nearly as strong as I was.

I didn't let her get very far when I backed away. "Kissing me won't keep me here."

Abby smirked. "Maybe something else will?" She got up onto her knees, giving me the amazing sight of her breasts.

I groaned. "Abby…" My voice was a warning.

She scrunched up her little nose. "You can't blame a girl for trying."

"No, I can't." I kissed her again. "And if I didn't have work, then your efforts would have been more than enough to keep me in bed all day."

"What will one day mean for a big CEO like yourself?" Despite her best effort, I wasn't going to change my answer. I couldn't.

Abby thought that when I said work, I meant going to the new publishing company I'd bought—the one she worked for. She probably thought I sat at a desk all day, reading reports and looking at manuscripts.

But I was used to excitement and sitting in front of a computer wasn't something I would enjoy. It also wasn't something my father would approve of. I needed the thrill of being in the mafia, the danger that came with each new day—the unknown that came with the power. Besides, the only reason that I'd even bought the business was because of Abby. I needed a way to get close to her, to be able to see her, and what better way than to be her boss? But at the end of the day, the place ran itself, and beyond keeping her employed, I didn't care about the publishing company.

Then again, had I known it would be this easy to convince her that I was worth her time, I might not have made the investment in the publishing company. After what she'd been through, I was sure there was going to be more of a challenge, and maybe with someone else, she might have put up more of a fight, but I was happy that she hadn't. It made things so much easier for me, and I was happy, truly happy, for the first time in my life.

"I have to go, Abby." My voice was stern. "Don't you have work, yourself?" I raised an eyebrow at her.

She groaned. "I guess you're right." Then those big eyes were back on me. "But you'll come back, right?"

I kissed her forehead. It was then that I saw how frightened she was. I didn't know if she was afraid of my not returning or what she had done and what it had meant to her—the connection we had made. Either way, I assuaged her fears. "Nothing could keep me away." And I meant those words. "But I do have to go."

"One more kiss." Her lips were insistent against mine, and I kissed her hard before pulling away.

I dressed, watching her as she lay in the bed, her eyes following me everywhere. Once I had my shoes on, I reached for her hand, kissed her fingers, and said, "Bye, babe."

There was a glimmer of sadness in her eyes, but I couldn't focus on it, or I wouldn't leave. "Bye," she murmured.

That one syllable nearly gutted me.

I took a second glance before I walked out of the bedroom and then the house. I had work I had to do, people I had to meet with, and God only knew what my father would say when he saw me. I had no idea if he would approve of Abby despite how much he had hammered on me to pick a wife. He probably wouldn't think she was a fit, not because she wasn't amazing, but because she didn't come from strong, Italian bloodlines and didn't carry a family name that would benefit our union, but I would make him see what I saw. I'd make him love her just as much as I did. And then he'd see how perfect she was, not just for me but for the family. She could be trained for her role; lots of women were.

WHEN I REACHED MY CAR, I slid inside and grabbed my cell phone from the cup holder. I'd left it there so Abby and I could have dinner uninterrupted. I hadn't planned not to come back out all night. As soon as I picked it up, I knew something important had gone down. I had multiple text messages from my father and several missed calls. I ran a hand through my hair before opening them.

My dad didn't bother me with business issues unless he needed my help. And my father didn't often admit when he couldn't do something on his own. But as he had aged, he had been drawing me in more and more, teaching me to step into his shoes as the future don.

When I finished reading the texts, I shot off a quick message telling him I was on my way and then put the car into gear. It didn't take me long to return to the mansion my family had lived in for generations.

A few more guards were posted than usual, who all nodded at me as I walked in. My father hadn't given me many details in the text messages and hadn't left any voicemails, but I could assume, from context clues, that something was wrong. That was the world mafia families lived in—there was always something wrong, always a battle being fought. We were just usually on the winning end of those wars, and we had been for generations.

"Where's my father?" I asked the guard.

He stood up straighter when he noticed who I was, as he should. He cleared his throat. "He's in his office."

"Thanks."

I went to my father's office and stood outside the door. Even though I was highly valued in our family, one person outranked me. And I knew better than to go in unannounced.

I knocked and waited for him to invite me inside. I didn't have to wait long.

"Come in," my father's gruff voice barked from the other side.

I opened the door, and my father was sitting at his desk with his glasses low on his nose. Another thing that age had taken—his sight. My father removed the glasses and stared at me, his hands clasped together in front of him. He didn't look pleased, far from it. Worse than that, there was a hint of disappointment in his eyes.

"Where have you been?"

Could I tell him the truth? "Why does it matter?" I asked and let out a breath. "I'm here now." It was disrespectful and I knew better, but damn, every aspect of my life was always open for evaluation, critique. And this was one area I wasn't going to give on—Abby.

"Is that the way that you talk to me?"

I let out a sigh. "My apologies."

"I'm sure you've gathered there's a reason I've called you here."

I took a seat in front of his desk and tried not to lounge the way I wanted to. Nothing irritated my father more than what appeared to be laziness, even if it wasn't. "Yes, I figured as much."

"One of my men," my father started but stopped himself and changed directions. "There's a traitor among us." He took this type of thing very seriously. Loyalty was the most important quality for anyone to possess who worked for us. "He's been trading our secrets to the Montero family. Our men have started to think we're weak. This perceived crack in our armor makes the other families believe they can divide us, that we're ripe for an attack. We need to remind them—the other families and our own men—of our power. Punish him. Torture him. Make him wish he hadn't been born."

He stared at me, letting what he'd just shared really sink in. I didn't ask who it was. I didn't need to—I'd see them when I walked into the warehouse. There was nothing more I hated in this world than a man I couldn't trust, especially when they were on my payroll. And my father knew that. He also knew that if he gave it just enough time to register that it would ignite a fire in me that wouldn't be extinguished until I'd exacted revenge for our family.

"I leave that task to you. I'm sure you can make better work of it than me, anyway."

He was right. It was a gift that I'd been given naturally; whether that was by God or the devil was arguable. But no matter how anyone looked at it, there was nobody who could torture someone better than I could. Everyone knew it—our men, other families—no one wanted to see me walk into a room when pain was coming. I'd inflict just enough to take them to the point of passing out, then I'd inject them with adrenaline to bring them back to endure more—over and over. I knew just how far I could take it before they died. And I never let their heart stop beating until I was ready to tear it from their chest.

I nodded. I understood the assignment. This wasn't one of the prettier parts of the job, but it was one I had to do. Whoever it was had broken the rules and, therefore, had to be punished. It was no secret among any of the families what happened to people who turned. And in our family, everyone knew I would be the one to dole out the punishment.

I was a monster. It was part of who I was, who I had to be. There was no doubt about it, and I wasn't going to argue about it, either. It was what was expected of me, and I was groomed for the job from an early age when my gift had been realized. I didn't shy away from that part of me, but I'd also never had a reason to before now. While I knew the truth, Abby didn't.

I could keep this part of my world a secret for the time being, but I wouldn't be able to hide it from her forever. I didn't want to think about what she was going to do when she found out the truth. I didn't know if the darkness I inflicted would be a deal-breaker or not. I had no idea what she'd do when she found out about the *real* me.

twelve

ABBY

THIS PAST WEEK had been the best I'd ever experienced. Being with Salvatore was a dream come true. In fact, it was almost too good to be true. He liked me for who I was, not who he wanted me to be. He accepted me as I was, despite my hesitations and quirks. Being with him should have been hard, considering my past, but it wasn't, which kind of scared me. It was the easiest thing that I'd ever done. I'd fully expected that I would have tons of first dates before I ever possibly found someone I would want to be in a relationship with after my ex-husband, but it was like Salvatore had been sent from God. It was the only explanation for my ability to let down my guard and Salvatore to walk past it.

Sometimes, I would find myself comparing Salvatore with my last boyfriend—or husband rather. He was the only man I'd ever been with. But there was no comparison. They were so opposite of each other that it was ridiculous. It made me wonder how I could have been attracted to both men when one was so incredibly wrong and the other so infallibly right.

But the attraction I felt for Salvatore was not the same attraction I'd felt for *him*. It was so much stronger, so much more real. When I wasn't with Salvatore, my thoughts were consumed by him. At all times, I wanted to be with him or near him. I was becoming obsessed, but I wasn't sure that was good.

But what could I do about it, now?

It wasn't like I could control the impulse, the constant desire. The only person Salvatore could blame was himself. He'd managed to fit into my life like a glove which was crazy to think about. He'd gotten me to lower my walls, drop my defenses. He'd encouraged me to fall for him. Until him, I'd grown accustomed to being on my own. I lived a very simple life. I woke up, showered, changed, went to work, came home, had a glass of wine, ate dinner, and went to sleep.

It was the same thing over and over again. Week after week. Month after month with little to no variation. I didn't even trust friends after everything Justin had done to me. And for months after he'd been taken into custody, every bump in the night made me jump, thinking he'd gotten out and had come to exact revenge on me. It was horrible, so I just stayed home where I was safe...or saf*er*.

Then Salvatore had come tumbling into my life and made me realize just how boring it'd been before. Yes, it was safe, but I wasn't living; I was merely existing. I couldn't imagine going back to that pathetic life. I had to acknowledge that I'd lived through hell in the past, but that didn't mean that I had to stay a victim forever. It was time for me to get my voice back, time for me to change my identity. I was resilient. I could be a phoenix, rise from the ashes of my past. Blaze into a new future.

And that seemed easy to do when I had Salvatore by my side. Then, there was our sex life. My teeth dragged across my bottom lip as I thought about it. It was incomparable, unmatched, immaculate. It was electric, the chemistry undeniable. I'd never felt anything like it before, and there wasn't any way that I was ever going to give it up, not willingly.

Salvatore could be as gentle as he was rough.

When we were in bed together, he fucked me like he hated me, as if I had done him wrong, like I was the enemy. And maybe that should have raised red flags for me, or I should have felt worse about myself. But I didn't. I liked it when he was rough. I preferred it. Did that make me a freak?

Outside of the bedroom, he was sweet, kind, and cared about me. It felt like he had more feelings for me than anyone else in my life. It was too soon to identify it as love, but damn if it didn't feel like it. Hell, maybe both of us were in this head over heels.

Well, there was no way I could say for sure. Although this week had been wonderful, I couldn't help but feel like he was hiding something. I didn't think Salvatore was a liar, but something was going on behind the scenes that he wasn't telling me. It could just be that, in actuality, we hadn't known each other long. Despite feeling totally consumed by him, I couldn't expect to know the ins and outs of every part of his life in a mere seven days. Hell, there were people who didn't know each other that well after seven *years*.

But I didn't like to be left in the dark, either.

Salvatore didn't seem to like to spend any more time away from me than I did from him. When he saw me, he was always so affectionate, telling me how much he had missed me and how much he wished he didn't have to go to work because he'd rather spend all of his time with me instead. Every word out of his mouth was genuine and heartfelt.

Was it weird that I believed him? Or, I had anyway.

Now, I wasn't so sure, and I was confident that it wasn't because of my past but rather how Salvatore was acting.

When he said that he was at work, I would call up to his office. And the weird thing? They'd say that he wasn't there, that he hadn't been there all day. I wanted to give Salvatore the benefit of the doubt, but how could I do that when it hadn't happened just once? It had happened every single time I'd called.

The first time I called his office wasn't because of any fear or suspicions. It was the exact opposite. I just wanted to talk to him, and if it led to phone sex, that was just a fun addition.

But Salvatore hadn't been there.

It had rubbed me the wrong way a little bit, but that hadn't had anything to do with him. Or, at least, I didn't think so. I wanted to blame it on my past, on the fact that I'd been lied to and betrayed more times than I could count. However, that didn't stop me from calling the next day. And then the day after that. And the results were always the same.

He wasn't at work. Or, at the very least, he wasn't in the office. But I couldn't imagine what he would be doing as the owner of a publishing company that wouldn't require him to be in the building, managing the business. The previous owner had been there—according to the rumor mill—even though I'd never met him.

So, where was Salvatore going, and why was he lying about it? In the short amount of time that we'd been dating, Salvatore constantly talked about the fact that he considered me "his" now. I belonged to him, and I didn't mind. It was nice feeling wanted and knowing that somebody cared. Actually, I found it incredibly arousing, and I'd be lying if I said it didn't play into my obsession with him.

However, I was just now realizing that the opposite had never been implied. I was his, but was he mine? I'd never asked him, nor had I said it. I'd always thought it was obvious, that it was reciprocated. But maybe there was a chance I'd been wrong, that all of what I believed was just in my head. It was possible that Salvatore held ownership to more than one woman around the city.

Maybe, we weren't as exclusive as I thought.

thirteen

ABBY

SALVATORE WAS the sexiest man I'd ever seen. He was far out of my league, and if he decided he wanted another woman, he could find one easily. There was nothing to stop him from cheating on me any more than any other man who'd ever walked the streets. The difference was that most men couldn't attract just *any* woman, and even fewer had the kind of wealth Salvatore clearly possessed.

It didn't take long for my thoughts to take a dark turn. *What am I going to do if Salvatore decides he no longer wants to be with me?* It was a reasonable question and one I needed to have answered. I'd only been with him for a week— seven days. I shouldn't feel this strongly about him, but I couldn't help myself. There was something about that man that pulled me in, like a current taking me out to sea. Once it had me in the undertow, I was helpless to resist. I didn't want to be away from him or think of this, of us, as anything other than permanent. But maybe I needed to open my eyes and be more realistic.

This thing between us could be nothing more than a phase, just sex. I didn't know if Salvatore wanted anything more than a fling. It was possible he was a playboy and I'd fallen for his charms.

Of course, it would break my heart if I invested in him this much just for him to tell me it hadn't meant anything to him. Nevertheless, I'd been in worse situations before. I would pick up the pieces and move on. I wasn't some fragile little girl my ex-husband had beaten and tortured anymore. I'd made myself a promise that I was going to be strong through everything. I would never resort to cowering or hiding in fear. I would stand up for myself and be a woman my parents would be proud of.

A man had nearly broken me once; I

wouldn't let the same thing happen again. I was falling for Salvatore, but that didn't mean that my life revolved around him, or any guy, for that matter. I was an independent woman who'd survived the flames and risen from the ashes.

Regardless of what happened with Salvatore and me, I would remain strong at the end of this. I was never going to allow another man to hold me back or crush my spirit. I was better than that, stronger than that.

My thoughts had wandered a thousand miles from where I was by the time I brought myself back to the present with the man in question lying next to me in bed, wrapped in his arms.

"Salvatore." My voice was low and husky.

We had just concluded another round of hot, passionate sex. I was exhausted and sweaty, and my head lay against his chest. He knew how to wear a girl out. Not that I was complaining. I couldn't think of anything better than sex with Salvatore, and I was pretty sure he knew as much. He wasn't terribly modest about his skills and abilities in the bed, but he had every right to boast.

"Hmm?" he hummed against me.

I had to do this. "Do you have work today?" Every part of me longed for him to say "no" that he didn't have to go to the office. And I wanted to believe him so badly, but I knew that I couldn't be that naïve, not with him.

Salvatore sighed. "Yes, I do," he whispered into my ear. "Although I wish I didn't because then, I'd be able to spend my entire day with you."

I wasn't buying it. "I don't have work today," I stated.

He rolled toward me a bit and lifted my chin to look into my eyes. "No?" he questioned. "Then, what do you plan on doing?"

"I thought I could visit you at the office for lunch," I suggested. "We've never had lunch together."

A fire was burning behind his eyes, and I could tell he knew something was off, different. But I wasn't going to back down. I'd backed down, all of my life, not again. I was going to get to the bottom of this.

"I'm sure you have better things to do than to come to the office on your off day," he stated. "After all, you do spend most of your time working." He petted my head and adjusted it back under his chin, essentially trying to end the discussion.

I smiled and tried to ease his concerns. "Yeah, but it doesn't feel like I'm coming to work. It would feel like I was visiting you, which makes it worth it." I didn't want him to get suspicious of my intentions. I looked back up at him, catching his eyes as I batted my lashes just a bit. "And I thought that maybe we could fulfill one of those fantasies of yours. I could take you in my mouth, under your desk, just like—"

Salvatore put a finger on my lips to stop me from continuing. "If you keep talking like that, I'll never leave."

"Then, don't."

"Not an option." Salvatore got out of bed. "Keep yourself busy, okay? And I'll see you after work."

He didn't give me a chance to say anything before he walked into the bathroom, closing the door behind him. I groaned and lay back down on the bed, feeling the frustration rise inside of me. It was clear, now. If it hadn't been obvious that he was hiding something before, then it was clear as day now.

I didn't listen to Salvatore's words. I watched the clock all day, with nothing better to do, and once it struck ten thirty, I drove over to the office. If he were there, I'd already rehearsed what I would say to him. I'd created an entire little story in my mind about why I was there, crafted it perfectly.

But my lie was unnecessary. I waited around at the office for Salvatore for hours, but he never showed up. And when I asked his secretary, a pretty and young woman I'd never met before today, she said he wasn't due to come in today, which put me back at square one. I'd had a feeling that he was lying, but now, I was sure. He was keeping a secret, and, from the looks of it, there wasn't a doubt in my mind that it was a big one.

I went back home and waited for him to return from work. Every horrible thought and possible scenario ran through my head in his absence, and I'd almost given up hope that he was even going to show. He was out late, far later than the owner of a publishing company would ever need to be. When I heard his car pull into the driveway, I made myself take a deep breath before I stared at the door.

Salvatore came in the same way he had for the last few days. He dropped his stuff in the entryway and hung up his suit jacket. He looked exhausted until his eyes latched onto me. "Abby," he said, my name relieved. "What are you doing? Were you waiting on me?" He grinned.

I almost believed the relief that flickered across his expression when he saw me. *Almost.* "Yes." I swallowed and feigned a smile. "Why are you here so late? I had given up hope that you were even coming. Where were you?"

He looked me dead in the eye. "I had a long night at work."

Liar.

SALVATORE

THE MORNING LIGHT was peeking through the blinds as I watched her sleep. I'd had to do a lot of distracting last night to avoid her questions because she was getting suspicious. It had been written all over her features when I had walked through the door. I should have known better than to think that she would believe my lies forever. Abby was a smart girl, and it was only a matter of time before she realized that not all of the puzzle pieces fit together. She had been in an abusive relationship, and she had gotten out of it. That meant one thing—she recognized bullshit from a mile away.

I had gotten myself caught in my spiral of deception with no way out of it.

Even if I could find a route out, I knew I didn't want to take it. This wasn't the kind of life I wanted to live with Abby. I wanted her to know everything about me, the *real* me, but how would she take the truth with the past that she had?

Her husband had been abusive. There was no way in hell she'd take kindly to finding out that her current boyfriend was a punisher, a torturer, and mafia boss by trade, and not the publishing house CEO I claimed to be. Although, that part wasn't a lie. I did own the company, and I was the CEO. I just wasn't an active employee who worked at the facility.

I would never lay a finger on Abby or raise a hand in anger, but she was the exception, not the rule. Any other person and I was a ruthless devil because that was the way I was. It was the way that I'd been born and raised. It was what made me the next in line for don.

My secrets weren't just for my protection, either. There were people out there who wanted to hurt me, and what better way to do that to a mafia member than to target his wife?

I loved Abby too much to put her in the middle of any drama or danger. She was too pure to be treated in such a rough way.

Part of me wanted to be the good guy she had fallen for. I knew I should leave her alone; I should have left her alone instead of pursuing her. She was too innocent for the world I belonged to, and she didn't need to be dragged down with me when things went bad. Lord knew I never wanted to tarnish anything about her.

But I wasn't a good guy. I was selfish, very much so at that. When I wanted something, I took it. And what I wanted was Abby. I'd gotten her, and there was no way that I was going to let her escape me.

My eyes trailed over her beautiful body, wondering if this would be the last time I got the chance to soak in her beauty. I'd already made up my mind. No more lies. I didn't know what the truth was going to bring, but I knew that it would change us—irrevocably. As much as I didn't want that, I didn't have a choice. She deserved to know who she'd gotten in bed with. I just prayed like hell she didn't want to leave once she knew the truth.

I trailed a finger along her cleavage and let out a deep breath. Her beauty was ridiculous. I could only imagine how envious the women around her were. Not to mention that I'd seen the looks men would give her when we walked past. But one hard glance from me, and they were changing the direction of their gazes.

And that was for the better. I'd killed men for less.

I pulled the bedspread down and allowed my eyes to feast on her breasts. But I could only look for so long before I got the urge to touch. Without a second thought, I leaned down and wrapped my lips around her tight, pink nipple, suckling hard. I wanted her to wake up and feel my tongue against her. I wanted her to be disheveled.

And she was.

Abby woke with wide eyes, looking around before her gaze fell on me. She relaxed, pushing backward and letting her hands claw at the sheets. She'd mentioned to me before how much she enjoyed it when I woke her up with my mouth. What could I say? I had a magical tongue.

I thrust a finger inside her waiting pussy. "Do you want me?" I asked her, my voice gruff.

She wasn't coherent enough to answer me, still sliding her ass around, refusing to stay still. Her motions told me the truth, but I wanted her words.

"Answer my question, Abby!" I curled my fingers inside of her, pleased when I heard her animalistic growl as I found the spot that turned her into a needy mess.

"Yes!" Her voice was breathy, the sexiest thing I'd ever heard.

She didn't even have to ask me. I pulled out my fingers, unzipped my slacks, took out my cock, and pushed my dick so deep into her that I was sure she could feel me in her throat.

She was almost crying as I pounded into her. I kissed her everywhere I could reach—her neck, breasts, cheeks, everywhere. Then, I lifted one of her legs, giving myself better access, as I continued to thrust in and out of her, wanting to make her feel me, not just my dick, but everything she meant to me. No matter what happened, I wanted her to feel me there tomorrow. Each step she took needed to be a reminder of who she belonged to—*me*.

Abby came, and I followed right after her, moving over to my side of the bed and struggling to catch my breath. I'd grown to love this little routine of ours, and I wasn't pleased with the thought that it might change.

I stripped out of my clothes, tossing them onto the floor next to the bed, and rolled over. Surprisingly, sleep took me quickly.

Breakfast the next morning was quieter than normal. If I weren't as clever as I was, I might have even thought everything between us was okay. But I knew better. I didn't know Abby's plan, but she had something in mind, and I wasn't a man who liked surprises.

"I'll see you tonight?" I said the words I always recited her before leaving for the day.

She smiled at me, but it didn't escape my attention that she hadn't answered the question.

Once I was on the road, it didn't take long to notice that she was following me. Abby was trying to be discreet, allowing for one car to be between us, thinking it would keep her concealed while also ensuring that she didn't lose me. Had she known who I really was, she would have realized this was a fruitless effort.

She couldn't be discreet enough for me not to catch on. My life depended on recognizing threats, even if they were harmless like they were in her case.

Maybe, I should have taken a separate route while I could. I should have pretended like I'd made the wrong turn and just taken the alternative way to work at the publishing company. But this wouldn't be over, and I didn't want to lie. How many times had she gotten to the work, looking for me only to find out that I wasn't there? That was a question I hadn't put much thought into before now.

I wasn't going to be able to throw her off, which meant I only had one option left.

I had to tell her the truth.

SALVATORE

SHE HAD to know what I did for a living, what family I came from. She could be in danger if she didn't. I just had to hope she was strong enough to handle the truth without freaking out or breaking down.

It was a risk, and I knew just how quickly things could go downhill, and then what was I going to do? I didn't want to let Abby go—I *wouldn't* let her go. That wasn't an option. Ever since I'd laid eyes on her the first time, I'd known she was going to be an integral part of my life, that she would change everything for me. And she had. I couldn't even begin to imagine a life that she wasn't involved in. We didn't live together, but I spent my days trying to get "home" to her, where I could fuck her and wake her up every morning with my tongue. Doing without that just wasn't a possibility—ever.

But what was I going to do if she decided that after seeing everything that I was capable of, she was no longer interested in me, wanted nothing more to do with me? And just how likely were those chances? The odds weren't in my favor, that was certain, and I didn't know how I would react if I heard her tell me that she no longer wanted to see me. It would be a devastating blow, and I really didn't think I'd adhere to her request anyhow.

I wasn't an emotional person, and not just because I was a man. My entire life, I'd been raised not to show how I felt because it could get me killed. It was a weakness, and everyone in my line of work sought out the weaknesses of others. They kept those little cracks in a database in their minds for when they needed to call upon them. And it happened—a lot. Weaknesses got lesser men than me killed. I'd always pushed it down because it was what kept me alive. But I didn't want to tamp it anymore, not with Abby anyway.

Keep her against her will. The thought flashed through my mind, but I knew I could never do that. She wasn't just some prisoner that I could do with as I pleased. She was the love of my life, and it wouldn't be the same if she didn't feel the same way about me.

So you're just going to let her leave you, then? I sighed as my eyes went to the rearview mirror. She was still two cars back, oblivious to the fact that I knew she was behind me. And, easily enough for her, all of her questions were about to be answered because we had arrived at our destination.

I'd debated taking her to the mansion where the entire mafia—the one I was a part of —would be.

Abby was strong, but I was certain she wouldn't be able to handle all of that. It was a lot to someone who had grown up in the life, much less someone who not only knew nothing about it but didn't know I was a part of it. So, instead, I brought her to our warehouse, the place where we would do only the dirtiest of deeds and hide our best weapons. But she wouldn't know. To Abby, this would be the extent of bad that I did. However, I wasn't going to let the truth end there. She wanted to know everything, and I was going to make sure she did. As the old saying went, curiosity killed the cat.

I went inside and closed the door behind me before standing on the other side, where I knew I wouldn't get hit when she stormed through it. I didn't have to wait long for the door to creak open slowly and Abby to slip inside, thinking she was disguised under the cover of darkness. But she couldn't be further from the truth.

I flicked on the lights and grabbed her arm. Immediately, she yelled and tried to pull away from me until she realized who it was.

"Salvatore," she said my name, reassured, at first, before her eyebrows furrowed into a frown, and she yanked away from me. "Salvatore! What the actual fuck are you doing here? And where is 'here?'"

I had to stop myself from laughing at her outburst because I knew the situation was about to get real, but it was ironic that she had trailed me and now acted like she hadn't been snooping or doing something mischievous. I'd let her out of this one because I loved her, but this shit would stop once she knew the truth. It wasn't safe for her to stick her nose into mafia business. The problem right now was that she had no idea I was tied to the mafia at all.

"I'm sure you have questions."

"I'm full of them."

"And, I'm going to answer them," I told her. "All of them."

She looked around. "I can assume you're not cheating on me then."

Not once in all the time I'd known she suspected something had I ever thought she'd questioned my fidelity. "No. Never." I shook my head to confirm that was a negative.

Abby moved on from that topic quickly, seemingly accepting my answer as the truth. "Why do you have so many guns?" There was no judgment or malice in her words, not even a hint of accusation, just pure curiosity.

"Because they're necessary for what I do." I could sense her fear as soon as I'd finished that sentence, and as much as I wanted to quiet it, I needed to let her feel the weight of what she was about to learn.

She cocked her head and stared me in the

eyes. "What does the owner of a publishing house need with all of these weapons?"

"Because I'm not just a book publisher, and I think you know that."

This was where her innocence came in, and I loved it and hated it all the same. "Then what are you?"

It was time for me to tell the truth. I didn't think pussyfooting or beating around the bush was the way to go. So I went straight to the heart of the matter. "I'm going to be the next leader."

Her confusion was written all over her face. She didn't need to speak for me to anticipate her next question. "Leader? Leader of what?"

I held her eyes, praying she could see how much I loved her. The next three words would decide my fate. "The Italian mafia."

Abby snorted. "Is that a joke?"

"No."

She was completely serious. "Do you... do you—?"

"Kill people," I finished for her. "Yes."

Abby's delicate hand flew to her mouth, her fingers covering the lips I longed to kiss. "Oh my God."

She started to run, but I grabbed her.

"Abby…"

"No! Let me go!" She pulled away and raced out of the building without giving me a second glance.

I'd done it. The truth was out. The question became, could I put all this back together now that she had all the pieces?

sixteen

ABBY

WHAT WAS WRONG WITH ME? I ran my fingers through my hair and tugged at the ends. I was close to losing it. I ripped my hands from my head and threw my head against the headboard. It had been days since I'd found out and I still didn't understand the thoughts going through my head. They didn't make sense.

The man I'd thought I could be in love with was nothing but a stranger to me. He'd been lying to me for days, leading me to think that he was a regular human being, living a normal life. But he wasn't. He was the leader of a gang, of the mafia—a criminal. Or, he was about to be, same difference.

The worst part of it all was the fact that he killed people for a living. It was a part of his job, and what did that even mean? He had it in himself to cause me—and anyone else—harm. After coming from an abusive relationship, I couldn't see myself being with another man who thought that hitting, killing, or violence, in general, was acceptable.

And even though I knew that, knew that he had the potential to kill me and not think twice about it, I missed him. Jesus, I missed the hell out of him. His touch, his kisses, his scent, his warmth—just *him*. Not being close to him was killing me. I'd grown accustomed to waking up in his arms. I had grown attached to this man in such a short period. Because he wasn't here, I felt empty inside. Lost and more broken than I'd felt when everything had ended with Justin.

He had lied to me, made himself out to be something he wasn't. Or had he? He had told me he was going to work every day, which he did, just not to the job I thought he'd meant. Shit—now I was justifying his behavior. There was something incredibly wrong with me. I'd gone from one type of abuse to another. I guess it was true that it was a cycle, one I hadn't managed to end. But my thoughts kept going back to him and the fact that I really didn't care what he did to anyone else as long as I was safe with him.

I didn't just want his love in my life. I needed *him*. I woke up every morning, hoping that his arms would be back around me and he'd be plunging deep inside of me. But it never came to be. Every morning was more of the same. Empty bed, no arms, and definitely no love. He'd done exactly as I'd asked him to; he'd left me to myself.

What was the point in wishing for anything? I'd given myself a false sense of hope, and now I was watching it erupt in flames. I was delusional to think that anything was going to change. Salvatore had walked out of my life just as easily as he'd walked in. What kind of mafia man does that? Don't they take what they want? Even against someone's will? Where was that side of Salvatore? Why wasn't he claiming me now? He'd said I was his but damn if he hadn't let me go without a fight.

But even if I wanted to change my mind, to be with a killer, then it wouldn't matter because there was no way for me to reach him.

He had made sure of that. It was like the second I had found out the truth, he'd decided he no longer wanted me and cut all ties.

I was the one who should have made that decision.

After what had happened with Justin, I never should have gotten involved with Salvatore. When I realized he was dangerous, I should have stayed far away from him. But it wasn't that easy. I'd felt this draw to him that I wasn't able to explain. When he'd come into my life, I'd felt like it was fate—kismet.

But now I knew differently. All of this had been an orchestrated plan carried out by Salvatore. And even knowing that, I still wanted to see him, even if it was just one more time, yet he still evaded me.

I didn't understand Salvatore. I didn't know why he'd chosen to be with me, why he'd started this dance. His buying out my publishing company was not just a coincidence. He'd done it to get close to me. *He'd* weaved his way into *my* life and had made *me* fall in love with *him*. He'd touched me tenderly like no other man had done before. He'd integrated himself into my life for a reason, with a purpose, so where the fuck was he now?

He'd dropped this bombshell on me and hadn't even bothered to stick around and explain it to me. Well, that wasn't exactly true. I had stormed out and told him to leave me alone, but I'd just needed some time to process. Now that I'd done that, I needed him and he was gone. He hadn't been to the office; his cell phone was disconnected—just poof, no more Salvatore. Every part of me believed he had played me, but I knew it was more than that. What we had was too real. It couldn't have been faked, not even by the best actors. I wasn't that naïve.

He had loved me just as I loved him. The fact that he'd told me the truth about who he was just confirmed that. He never would have revealed that to just anyone. And it didn't matter what he'd done or what he was doing. I could accept all of his secrets and all of his flaws if that meant that I got to be with him. I'd find a way to overlook the bad parts of his job—they were just things he did; it wasn't who he was. At least, it wasn't who he was when he was with me, and that was all that mattered. I never thought that I'd care so much about someone again, but it looked like I was wrong. There was no way I was going to be able to let him go.

But it was too late now.

I'd come to this realization much too late because Salvatore was gone.

He'd disappeared from my life without a trace, without a way for me to reach him. All of his stuff was gone, and it was like he'd never been a part of my life to begin with. How could he be so much like a ghost? I was sure that in a few months, this would all feel like some dream, but that was the last thing I wanted. I had no desire to erase the man I loved from my memory.

I wanted back what I had lost.

MY LAST-DITCH EFFORT was going back to the warehouse where everything had gone down, where everything had gone wrong. I drove furiously as if my life depended on it. The outside looked the same as it did the day I was there, and all I could do was hope that the inside would as well.

But my hopes were crushed once again. Everything was cleared out. His ghost had swept through there, as well. I allowed myself to break down at the truth. The tears ran down my cheeks, and I couldn't stop the sobs from leaving my lips.

That was it. Salvatore had broken up with me. Left me. Abandoned me for good.

There were no traces of him. He'd made it clear what he had wanted. If Salvatore had cared to talk to me, he would have left me with a way to contact him. This was his way of severing all ties, ending it once and for all. There was no way I could doubt that anymore. I couldn't keep lying to myself when the truth was staring me dead in the eye.

Salvatore didn't want me. He'd left me, and there was nothing I could do about it. I'd told him to leave me alone, and instead of fighting for, chasing after me, begging me to listen, he'd just let me go.

All I did was sulk in my room for days until I heard that the publishing company was being sold again. That was the one thing I needed to give me hope again. Salvatore had to return to sell the company, and I would be there when he did. I got myself out of bed and drove to the office quicker than I should have, frightened I would get a ticket and be slowed down.

Thankfully, I wasn't caught. The cops were more focused on other things, which allowed me to arrive without any issues. I did the best I could to look up and then search the parking lot, noting that his car was there. Salvatore was in the building. My heart did a weird skipping thing before it started to race and my cheeks flushed.

Before I went to the nineteenth floor, I stopped in the bathroom in the lobby. I stared at myself in the mirror, and I noted I didn't look like myself. My hair was wild, and there were dark circles under my eyes. It was obvious I hadn't slept in days, and, quite frankly, homeless people looked better kept than I did in my present state.

Without giving it a second thought, I opened the bathroom door and quickly walked to the elevator, not bothering to take in my surroundings. I needed to get to Salvatore before he left. This could be my last chance.

I couldn't believe that I was about to walk into the office in such a tousled state, but I didn't have another option. I had been using my sick days, so I didn't have to come to work, and I was out of time.

My first instinct was to go to his office. Where else was I going to go? The secretary greeted me at the door with a puzzled expression, but I didn't say anything back. I had other things on my mind that were more important.

I didn't bother knocking. I opened the door, and there was Salvatore, shaking hands with a guy I didn't know, who had to be the man who'd bought the company. He looked surprised to see me there, but he hid it well.

"Who is this?" the stranger asked in confusion.

"Someone from my past," Salvatore answered. "I'll be in contact via email."

"Sounds good."

The man left, leaving Salvatore and me alone together, just like it needed to be. The door closed, and I swallowed.

"Why?" I asked him, trying to be strong, and when he didn't answer, I repeated myself a little louder. "Why?"

"Why, what, Abby?" he asked me, raising an eyebrow as if I were the one who was being unreasonable.

"Why did you leave me?"

He blanched like I'd hit him. "You left me, Abby."

I frowned. "What the fuck are you talking about?"

"Wow," he chuckled. "Look at you getting

some fire underneath those old bones. That was what I always wanted for you."

"Be serious for one second, Salvatore!"

"I loved you!" he roared. "And what did you do? You found out the truth, and you decided you didn't want me. You told me to let you go, and the look in your eyes told me that was truly what you'd wanted. You would have made the same decision to stay away."

"No, I wouldn't have," I argued, feeling myself getting emotional. "Because I love you. I love you more than anything else in this fucking world, and you decided to leave me without a trace just because I needed some time to process what you'd dumped on me. Is that really what you want? Do you want me out of your life? Because if you say the word right now, I'll drop this. I'll let it go. I'll let *you* go. It'll be the hardest thing I've ever had to do, which is saying a lot, but all you have to do is tell me once. What do you want?"

The tears were pouring down my face, and Salvatore stared at me before letting out a deep breath.

"I choose never to let you go again."

He walked toward me and wrapped his

arms around me before crushing his lips against mine. I cried into the kiss, my hands immediately going to his hair and tugging violently on the strands. He felt so good against me, and I realized just how much I had missed him and his affection.

Salvatore pulled away. "No more running, no more staying away," he whispered to me. "You're always going to be by my side—always. Be mine forever. Marry me, Abby."

I didn't have to think hard about it. "Yes."

He smiled. "Really?"

"Yes!" I jumped into his arms while I kissed him.

epilogue

SALVATORE

THERE WAS a loud knock on the door, and I sighed. I stopped what I was doing for a moment and heard my fiancée let out a loud and disappointed sigh. Abby frowned at me, and I couldn't help but laugh. My girl was never satisfied, but getting interrupted was frustrating for anyone.

"Oh, my sweet, Abby," I whispered against her pussy. "Are you horny?" I let out a small breath against her clit right before I sucked it one last time, and I could see her biting into that plump, bottom lip. Fuck, everything about her turned me on—hence the reason we were in the situation we currently found ourselves.

"Of course, I am. Look what you're doing," she whined. "Please, don't stop!" Her expression was what had put me down here in the first place. She knew I'd never turn her down.

I'd been eating her out with zero remorse, something she was quite used to by this point. My tongue had been swirling around her sensitive pearl, and now, it was obvious that she wanted that back. She hadn't finished, and I didn't want to quit. Abby had always enjoyed the feel of my tongue against her delicate folds, and I couldn't deny how much I loved her taste and the way she moaned my name each time I dipped a finger into her tight hole. And I was certain the only thing she was upset about was the fact that I had stopped.

I wanted to finish what I was doing, but I doubted that would be the answer. We had known how high the chances were that we weren't going to finish this when we'd started; neither of us cared. And we had decided to forge ahead anyway. We had nobody to blame but ourselves and our insatiability. Abby always wanted me as much as I did her, and we rarely let anything stop us when the mood hit.

"I have to stop, Abby," I told her even though she was clearly unhappy with my response. I wanted to give her everything she ever wanted—including her next orgasm—but sometimes, that wasn't an option. Right now was one of those times. "We can't be late for our wedding."

"Says who?" Abby asked, being dramatic as if she were a child. "It's *our* wedding. It won't start until we get there." She rolled her eyes, her legs still spread wide before me and her dress hitched up around her waist—fuck her wet pussy was gorgeous.

"Abby..." I warned her.

She sighed and sat up, giving in to our fate. She pulled down her wedding dress, and I thought about how beautiful she was clothed as well as naked. I wanted to ravage her all over again.

I kissed her pouty lips one more time, knowing that tasting herself on my mouth drove her crazy. "We should get ready to go."

"Fine," she rolled her eyes. "You know, technically, this is all your fault. We wouldn't have had the chance to even do naughty things if you hadn't burst in here like some madman.

You're not supposed to see your bride before the wedding, don't you know that? It's supposed to bring all kinds of bad luck."

"I'd rather have bad luck than go through one day without seeing you." It was the truth, not just some canned line.

I had gone my entire life without her, and I didn't plan on going another second. Today was the day that she would officially become mine. The one where my last name would become hers. It was going to be a day to remember.

We got up from the small couch in her dressing room. I stood, and she fluffed out her dress before wrapping her arms around my neck. She smiled at me and leaned upward so our lips could press against each other. When she pulled away, she smiled at me. "It's about time for you to be all mine—finally."

"Oh, trust me, Abby," I started, "I always was."

That woman had no idea just how she had truly owned me since the moment she'd run into me. I'd moved heaven and earth to be with her, and I'd do it all again just to get to this moment.

We kissed one more time, and I knew I was ready to start my life with her forever.

Click or scan the QR code to check out other books by Mila Hart

acknowledgments

To the three of you who buy our books, we love you! To the rest of you cunty whores, thanks for nothing, bitches. Just kidding, if you're reading this, I guess you bought the book, so you're being added to the three afore-mentioned.

It all started with two best friends and a whole lot of dirty ideas...

MILA HART is your go-to for cheeky, steamy, and seriously spicy reads. We're all about quick, hot stories that get your heart racing and leave you wanting more—but here's the twist: we give you both the heat and the story.

With tons of deliciously sexy tales in the works, get ready for the perfect mix of plot and passion—because we're just getting started!

Check us out at:
www.authormilahart.com

9 7 9 8 2 2 7 7 7 8 1 4 7